THE STRANGE MUSEUM

THE STRANGE MUSEUM

50-WORD STORIES

RAN WALKER

ISBN 9781020001161 (Paperback)
ISBN 9781020001178 (Ebook)
Library of Congress Control Number: 2020900747
First Edition

10 9 8 7 6 5 4 3 2

www.45alternate.com
45 Alternate Press, LLC
Hampton, VA

CONTENTS

*For all of the librarians out there
who continue to fight the good fight*

FOREWORD

Ran Walker and I are music fans. We debate our top five MCs, favorite albums, and favorite producers. During one debate, we were going on and on about The Foreign Exchange's then-recent release, *Authenticity*. I was impressed with the music, yet Ran was more impressed with something else, something I had never considered in an album. He was impressed with the album's run time—its efficiency.

My favorite album, Isaac Hayes's *Hot Buttered Soul*, only has four songs and I didn't think an artist could get more efficient than that. But The Foreign Exchange did and, more importantly, Ran's appreciation for word economy was beginning to bloom.

Shortly afterwards, he expressed a discontent for the novel format, saying it was too long. Going forward, he pledged allegiance to the novella. Then the novellette became his medium of choice. Eventually, he became enthralled with the possibilities of short stories. Later, he became a devotee of flash fiction.

The first time I heard of most of these mediums was through our conversations. Conversations that were longer than most of his writings. Discussions that revolved around artist and artistry. Creative exchanges that revealed his preference for word efficiency.

It came as no surprise when he wrote a book of Kwansabas (poems with seven lines with seven words each and no word longer than seven letters). It seemed that with each medium his word count lessened, while the imagery became more vivid.

His retraction of forms has come to this: a micro-fiction collection of one hundred 50-word stories.

Yet, as you will find, *The Strange Museum* is really more than one hundred stories. Because for every story read from the page, another story is sparked in the mind, a sort of creative alchemic formula that Ran has mastered: the ability to create more with less.

Sabin Prentis, January 2020

INTRODUCTION

They have been called everything from dribbles to mini-sagas (a phrase coined by *The Daily Telegraph*) to microstories to ultra-short stories, but in the end, they all mean one thing: 50-word stories. These stories are meticulously crafted and edited so that the entirety of the story and the universe that is implied comes through in the selection of the right fifty words.

Admittedly, I became familiar with the concept of writing 50-word stories when I stumbled across Tim Sevenhuysen's online literary journal, *50-Word Stories*. I became intrigued with them, mainly because the University of Hell Press had just published a collection of my Kwansabas. Kwansabas (the brainchild of Dr. Eugene Redmond) are forty-nine word poems (seven lines, seven words per line, and no word of more than seven letters). I figured writing a story of fifty words just meant that I'd have to add one more word.

I was wrong.

The thought process behind writing fifty-word stories is a bit different from the process I employed to write Kwansabas. For one, narrative is far more important. How can you possibly tell a story that contains a beginning, middle, and end in a rather thin paragraph? In this regard, fifty-word stories do take a few cues from poetry. To write stories this short, you have to use certain words to evoke things greater than themselves. Each sentence has to be resonant. The reader must also be able to engage with the story enough to supply the information that is not actually on the page. So like poetry, fifty-word stories demand to be read a bit slower than normal short stories.

These stories run the gamut: fables, dark suspense, humor, and vignettes from everyday life. As you read them, you will find that they rest at the intersection of flash fiction and prose poetry, a sweet spot where, for just a few minutes out of a day, you can completely lose yourself in a story.

So without further ado, I welcome you to *The Strange Museum*. Enjoy your time here.

Ran Walker, January 2020

"Brevity is the sister of talent."

— ANTON CHEKHOV

WELCOME TO THE STRANGE MUSEUM

FIFTY WORDS

When the idea first struck the writer, he thought it would make for an amazing novel, but as the idea settled, he considered a novella more apt. Then a novelette, short story, flash fiction, and microfiction.

But the idea finally came alive when he wrote it down in fifty words.

PURPLE

Wallace sat on a bench in the garden, a bag of Skittles in his hands. The EnChroma glasses were a gift from his grandchildren. They'd asked him to identify colors he was only recognizing for the first time.

Now alone, he sat gazing at the English violets, lost in purple.

MORE ROBOT, PLEASE

Initially the thought of owning a sex robot that "looked human" felt like a good idea. After weeks of looking into its eyes, though, Norman felt judged, as he'd been in his previous relationships.

Using his warranty, he sent it back to the factory in favor of one less human.

BUTTER ME UP

It was only after Mrs. Fennelly's prize-winning butter sculpture "A Day in the Life of My Family" was carefully melted that the clean-up crew at the Iowa State Fair discovered the likenesses of her four family members were the result of her having actually used each of her family members.

5

———

HE'S COMING

Those who could run, ran.

Those who could hide, hid.

The rest of us hunkered down to fight, fists squeezing chair legs, staplers, keyboards, waste-baskets, anything we could find.

As the loud popping sound drew closer, we exhaled slowly and did our best to prepare for what was to come.

6

____

AN EPILOGUE

The owners complained they no longer had the time—with marriage, kids, and life in general—and could no longer afford to operate a business with such slim margins, but when the time came to officially close its doors, none of them could bear to let the old bookstore go.

ODE TO AN OLIVETTI

For sixty-five years, the writer conversed back and forth with her typewriter, its keys creating a bridge to her imagination.

When arthritis stiffened her fingers and her mind began to wander, the typewriter kept right on telling those stories, willing itself to become the voice for the two of them.

THE MONSTER

Sometimes the debt would appear as a massive sinkhole in the living room floor, one into which he dreaded he might one day dive, to be chewed up and consumed within the abyss of its distended belly, the monster's savage lips smacking sharply somewhere miles above.

Sometimes he ignored it.

THE WAYS WE SAY GOODBYE

They made love before he took her to the airport. Her student exchange had ended, but she vowed to keep in touch. He promised the same.

They sat in his car, holding each other tightly, knowing that once she boarded her flight, they would only be left with that memory.

HICKORY

*K*en believed our scoutmaster when he said adding dry leaves would give the stew a nice "hickory" flavor. We couldn't stop Ken in time to keep all of the leaves out, but when we won first prize for "Best Camporee Meal," no one mentioned the secret ingredient to the judges.

ONOMATOPHOBIA

They had navigated their entire courtship without using their names. She was particular, so they stuck with pronouns. Eventually they had a child, at which point a name had to be written down.

They chose Baby, but even that name would drive her crazy for the rest of her days.

12

THE SMILE

The idea arose when Sophia's father said her smile was more beautiful than Mona Lisa's. After retiring from the grade school, she used her savings to go to Paris, where she wandered the Louvre until she found it. Staring at Leonardo's masterpiece, she could only think, "Wow. It's so *small*."

THE KISS

While Terrance stood on the corner of Third and Main, a random beautiful woman grabbed him, kissing him passionately, before profusely apologizing and walking away.

Later that night he considered two distinct possibilities: either there was a doppelgänger of him out there somewhere or he was simply a lucky man.

UNTIL THE END OF TIME

The other owners at the dog park eyed Stonewall curiously, attempting to make sense of the dog's ticking movements. Ian welcomed the attention. Only another skilled horologist would understand the complex automatic movement, and only someone who'd buried one too many beloved dogs would understand his need to build one.

FATHERHOOD

*B*ack before his daughter was born, he evaluated movies objectively, as if he were some kind of unpaid movie critic. When she arrived, though, he found that even a cartoon about a clown fish searching the ocean for his only son could leave him wiping the corners of his eyes.

THE GOAT

he producers of the TV game show had to explain to Njomo that the goat behind Door Number Three was intended as entertainment to illustrate his having lost the game, not a cherished award to be taken back home to his village and used as a dowry for his bride-to-be.

THE BAGPIPE LESSON

alcolm gazed at Tanner's *The Bagpipe Lesson*. He had learned playing the bagpipes was once illegal, just like black people learning to read in America. It seemed funny that the painting would be at Hampton University, but Malcolm smiled, swearing if he listened hard enough he could hear the chanter.

THE STORY THEY WOULD ONE DAY TELL THEIR CHILDREN

She had attempted to ignore him, hoping he wouldn't approach her as she stood alone on the aisle of the bookstore. He was the persistent kind, though.

After approaching her, he mustered a polite smile and blinked twice.

"Excuse me," she said by way of introduction, gently fanning behind herself.

REVERENCE

ecause Jeremiah's great-great-great-grandfather was not executed for treason after the Great War, his family spoke of the man as a hero for the next few generations to the point Jeremiah had hung a huge replica of the flag for this lost cause above his own mahogany mantle in deep reverence.

THE DEFAULTS OF OUR IMAGINATION

When Dorian gave his acceptance speech, he casually revealed the characters of his novel were African-American. He went on to point out the symbolism and signifyin' the judges had failed to notice.

Handing him his award, they struggled to mask their embarrassment that they had never truly understood his book.

21

A PARTY OF ONE

*S*abrina spent her twenty-fifth birthday scrolling through her social media feeds, checking for birthday wishes from her friends and followers. Once she had responded to all of their messages, she posted a picture of her designer birthday cake, before tossing it in the trash and crying, alone, in her apartment.

PLIERS AND FAIRIES

nemployed and strapped for cash, Jake remained vigilant about getting the money for his daughter's prom dress.

When he woke the following morning to find several crisp one hundred-dollar bills beneath his pillow, he forced a smile and tried to ignore the throbbing in the clotted sockets of his gums.

HUNTING MONSTERS

Two unexpected things happened after Timmy killed the monster under his bed: (1) he ate it (and rather enjoyed it), and (2) he took to hunting the monsters under the beds of other neighborhood kids. After all, someone had to do it—and he'd already developed a rather insatiable appetite.

A METAMORPHOSIS IN HARLEM

On the morning after Kendrick read Kafka for the first time, he woke to find he had in fact turned into a giant cockroach. Shortly afterwards, his girlfriend, Patricia, unloaded an entire can of Raid on him, before proceeding to beat him to death with every shoe in her closet.

NESSIE

There is a large serpent that lies 700 feet down in the belly of the loch, tucked away in some dark crevice, its belly swollen, full with the many rumors of its existence. When it belches, the bubbles of our hopes rise through the darkness to rest at the surface.

A FISH TALE

The observer told Jonah the thing that had swallowed him was a wels catfish.

"Surely it was a *whale*," Jonah said.

"You were swallowed by a great fish, and a whale isn't a fish."

Jonah considered this. "But they'll still call it a whale."

"Perhaps. But it was a catfish."

HOW TO TRAIN A BEAST

The first time the beast came to the village was by accident. He had simply lost his way. However, once he learned the townspeople were willing to feed him one of their own each year, gradually incorporating more festivities and rituals into his visits, the beast vowed to keep returning.

THE UNPAID DEBT

The townspeople of Hamelin spent the afternoon fishing the bodies of 130 children from the Weser River. One by one, their bodies were pulled ashore, the mayor's own son among the lot.

"If only I had paid the pied piper," he muttered—but that would have been a different tale.

A NECKLACE

(AFTER GUY DE MAUPASSANT)

The diamond necklace Mrs. Taylor borrowed was either real or it wasn't, but she wore it to the party, lost it, then lied about losing it, before purchasing a new necklace, which may or may not have been real, depending upon which author you ask, to return to her friend.

AN UNEXPECTED GIFT

The family had been starving all winter, so they were relieved when the siblings returned with a large hunk of smoked meat. Standing around the table, they blessed the food, then asked the two to come forward and carve the first pieces.

"Hansel and Gretel, would you do the honors?"

PLAN B

The little girl used the last of her magic to cast a fog over the village, in hopes the soldiers would not discover them. As the undeterred men moved closer, though, she reluctantly turned loose the wild boars that tore through the mist, ravenously gnawing at ankles and drawing fire.

THE MOTIVE

The North Pole Police found Jolly the Elf hiding underneath a snow-covered tarp behind the old toy factory.

At the precinct they asked him repeatedly, "Why did you do it?"

Looking down at his blood-stained crakows, Jolly finally said, "Why should *he* get to have all the milk and cookies?"

THE DOMESTICATED GETAWAY

G ary leaped up through the brush, going as fast as his little legs could take him. If he were as wild as his cousins, he would've flown.

The President only pardoned one turkey. For the rest of them, it was open season, and Gary had no plans of getting caught.

A NEW YEAR WITHOUT GRANDMA

"Don't forget," Mom warned me.

"I won't."

Grandma Jo had been cremated and didn't want a funeral. She'd only asked for us to toast her at midnight.

Glass in hand, I accidentally dozed off, but the cacophony of fireworks woke me just in time to raise my glass in remembrance.

A CHRISTMAS SONG

Every time Will performed one of his Christmas concerts at the old club, he wondered about what had brought each audience member in that particular evening. Was it the music? Was it him? Or maybe it was just that they, too, longed to be connected to someone during the season.

THE MAGICAL BOOK

Zora discovered that the book her grandmother had given her was a multiverse key. She went back and forth in time, altering history, trying to right wrongs, until she could no longer tell which reality was her own.

In every version someone lost or won, but peace was always elusive.

AND THE WHEELS OF TIME KEEP TURNING

The old man continued to pedal on weary legs, his motion the only thing keeping the hands of the Great Clock moving. Slowly the tower door opened.

A girl of no more than eight walked in.

"You're the Angel of Death?" he asked.

"No. I have come to replace you."

THE THING I HAD TO DO

"I can't believe you just did that."

"But you deserved it. You had to have seen it coming."

"That's not the point. It was just so unnecessary."

"You pushed me into a corner. What would you have done?"

"The same thing, I guess. Still you didn't have to do it."

WRAITH

On Halloween she revealed she was leaving him for another man.

"I'll stop eating," he warned, hoping to stop her.

She left anyway, so he stopped eating.

Days later when she returned for the last of her things, he'd already wasted away, a wraith without the strength to haunt anyone.

YOU CAN NEVER LEAVE

The disheveled man sat on the corner, his worn guitar resting on his lap while he sang "Hotel California," the raspiness of his voice pushing through the thick beard on his face. For a moment people stopped, mesmerized. When he finished, though, people continued on as if he'd never played.

LOVE HAS NO LIMITS

*B*en purchased the mathematics textbook at a yard sale. A high school dropout, he was amazed at how the numbers spoke to him. Geometry, Algebra, and Calculus —all in a year. Although he vowed to never re-marry after his wife died, he hoped she would allow him this one love.

STAY

He struggled to ignore the yelling outside his window, as he cradled the phone against his ear. Some of his constituents would hate him, he knew, but he now had doubts and didn't want to have to explain himself to St. Peter.

"Governor?" asked the correctional officer on the line.

THE MOURNER

She'd been hired for that first funeral, just someone to mourn a poor soul who'd died without family or friends. After her own family began passing away, she started doing the funerals for free. Maybe if she did enough, she figured, someone might do the same for her one day.

SUPER EXPECTATIONS

Yvette had known she could fly weeks before she flew up to rescue the boy. It was like MJ and the Moonwalk. He had worked on the step for three years before he unveiled it at Motown 25.

While her feat wowed everyone, Yvette was underwhelmed by her superhero debut.

STONE WINGS

Cynthia hadn't noticed the striking similarity between herself and the statue of the angel in Dewald's Cemetery. Her friends, though, made much of it, the way teenagers sometimes do, posting collages of Cynthia and the angel online.

That night Cynthia dreamed she could flap her stone wings and fly away.

HITCHHIKERS

Mother warned her about picking up hitchhikers on a full moon, but it was only when the man sat down that Amy understood why.

Amy struggled to steer, as her claws grew. The man screamed, and Amy, now starving, snapped at the man as the car leaped into the darkness.

THE SCARECROW

*J*erry fought the peer pressure from his friends to pelt the old scarecrow with miniature pumpkins they had stolen from Old Man Granger's farmer's market. That was why when Halloween night finally arrived and the battered scarecrow stepped down from its perch, Jerry was the only one who was spared.

DANCING IN THE LIGHT

Frank hated the idea, but a mother in his support group said it had been helpful.

So he set it up in Jessica's old room and attempted to steel himself.

When they discovered Frank's emaciated body, his frozen smile was still fixed on the flickering hologram of his daughter dancing.

BEHIND HIS BACK

Shortly after Greg woke to discover his vertebrae had permanently fused with his wife's while they'd slept, he became curious if she had been complaining to her friends about him behind his back.

When she awoke screaming, desperate to pull away from him, he smiled, realizing it didn't matter anymore.

PEOPLE ARE STRANGE

Shortly before the museum opened, the humans came out of their rooms and assumed their places behind each exhibit sign. The Venusians filed in one at a time to gawk at them. It wasn't exactly a treaty, but this arrangement had, up till this point, managed to prevent interplanetary war.

EXHIBITS CONTINUE THIS WAY

FIFTY WORDS

When Nia learned that her grandmother's grandmother had been an enslaved woman who had made it her goal to learn to write fifty words—during a time when slaves could be put to death for reading or writing—she vowed to spend the rest of her life writing fifty-word stories.

PURPLE

On their first date, she told him her favorite color was purple.

He responded, "Mine, too!"

Surely this meant something, they thought, staring at each other.

Neither had dated in over a year, so, silently, they agreed to let their love of purple be suitable grounds for a second date.

THE MIDNIGHT DANCE

In the pitch-black darkness of the woods, long, slender trees danced, their branches interlocking like fingers, as they moved the earth with their roots, pushing and pulling the land like a DJ scratching a record.

The townspeople claimed the woods were haunted, but they were wrong. The woods were *happy*.

THE MONSTER INSIDE

*W*hen the zombie apocalypse arrived, Jack was trapped inside a bookstore, staring at the manager, even though she'd once told him she would only date him if he were the last man on earth. As the undead clawed at the windows from outside, a dark smile formed upon Jack's lips.

WITNESS

*T*itus wanted his father to be proud of him, so he tagged along. He'd heard of lynchings before, but had never seen one.

When he returned home later that night, he could still hear the man's screams, and he knew those screams would haunt him until the day he died.

PDA (PUBLIC DISPLAY OF ANGER)

The woman stood outside the cell phone store screaming obscenities and shaking her ponytail back and forth, as if she were fighting with herself, but then I caught glimpse of her AirPods. I thought that would have made me feel more comfortable about her public display—but somehow it didn't.

LIMITED EDITION

*I*t didn't matter that I'd waited in line all night and saved for months to buy them.

"Run those kicks!" the kid repeated, waving his gun.

I could hear Mom's voice in my head: "No shoe is worth your life."

So I stepped out of them onto the cool pavement.

BREAK-UP/BREAK-DOWN

The crude handlebar mustache appeared on Evan's face after Lane drew on the old funhouse photo with a marker. He begged her to stop, even apologized for cheating, but his apologies couldn't mend her broken heart.

She crumpled the picture and tossed Evan into the trash on the way out.

BEWARE

*W*ord had spread to all the mischievous kids in the subdivision that Mr. Hanks had a sign on his back fence that read "Beware of Cassowary." Although none of them had seen one, beyond Google images, they decided right then to stick with houses that only had dogs guarding them.

THE END

The alien discovery divided the town: they wanted to eat it or screw it or deify it or kill it just to see what would happen. What they didn't know was that it was a scout sent to determine if humans should be annihilated, and that they'd failed the test.

OUR CHILDREN ARE GENIUSES

The Morrises took pictures of Little Josh's popsicle splatterings on the summer pavement and placed them on the refrigerator. When visitors came over, the Morrisons would say, "Looks like a Jackson Pollock, right?"

Out of courtesy, guests usually responded, "Yes."

"Well, our three-year-old has the uncanny skill of Jean-Michel Basquiat."

FRIDAY NIGHT PARTYING

We floated into the third club of the night, still riding the liquid courage from the cheap drinks three doors down.

Women appeared from nowhere, and we danced out the last of the alcohol.

In the end, I left with a fake number, and my boy Jeff left with mono.

FIREWORKS

My science class didn't know what to make of the strange explosion on TV. Then someone told us the space shuttle had exploded.

It would be decades later when I learned the astronauts actually died when their capsule slammed into the ocean. Still, I imagine them in midair, like fireworks.

A LITERARY CONFERENCE

The novelist, who had been invited to the conference as a special guest, sat back, listening to the scholars dissect, analyze, and praise his work. When they finally addressed him to ask his intentions surrounding a bit of literary minutiae, he politely responded, "You would know far better than I."

WHAT LIES AHEAD

aith had been in line for what felt like years, waiting to meet the Ultimate. Eventually whispers from farther up in the line arrived with news that there was no Ultimate.

Discouraged, many people left the line to embrace the Nothingness. Faith, however, stayed put, too afraid of being wrong.

**

$\mathcal{B}$aron had been counting the days until retirement, fantasizing about the adventures he'd go on when he didn't have to operate the old machine anymore.

But when the day finally arrived, he was exhausted and found he'd rather sit on his La-Z-Boy recliner and watch everything from his fifty-inch flatscreen.

REAL MAGIC

Lisa became a magician's assistant because she thought she would learn how to disappear. She soon learned it was all trap doors, hidden compartments, and smoke and mirrors, though.

She would have to learn to create her own form of "Black Girl Magic" and become comfortable taking refuge within herself.

THE FAIRY KING

*A*rthur intended every aspect of his book to be literal, but the critics who fell in love with it spoke of it as a parable, an allegory for the times. He was lauded for his ingenuity, but never in the book's multiple printings did anyone consider that fairies were *real*.

INFINITY

*A*ttempting to be funny, Sherman asked our eccentric math professor what "infinity" was. The professor smiled and took a piece of chalk and drew a line around the room fifty times, before dragging it past the classroom door, down the long corridor, to his car.

We never saw him again.

LITERAL INTERPRETATIONS

One morning Vanessa went to brush her teeth, and one by one they tumbled into the sink. Her nightmares had come true, she thought, wiping away the blood. She moved her lips over her gums, looking at her ninety-year-old face in the mirror. For the first time, she felt old.

PARCHMAN

o matter how "dangerous" a guy he was or how much he benched on the yard or who he had to hem up during the day or how long he'd been without a letter from his old lady, Deebo laughed like a child whenever he watched Betty White on TV.

DEFECTIVE

Dear Customer Service:

I'm returning the gremlin I ordered because it's defective. I've taken it on cars, planes, and even boats, and there hasn't been a single incident of mischief.

If you could send me a new one or refund my money, I would greatly appreciate it.

Sincerely,

R. Dahl

COVER YOUR EYES

There were rumors the film was cursed, that there'd been a death on the set, that one of the actors had committed suicide, that an editor had gone crazy compiling the final mix.

I refused to watch it—which is why I'm the only one left to tell this story.

TOMBSTONE RUBBING

At night they tip-toed into the cemetery with their tools, camping out at celebrity headstones, carefully copying the engraved text from weathered surfaces, hands restless with exploration.

Once they finished, they tucked away their work and eased out into the night, their brush with greatness still tingling on their fingertips.

NOVEMBER 4, 2008

We rushed out into the streets, where we were swept along in the growing crowd, celebration erupting from our lips to join the chorus, tears streaming down our faces.

We danced outside the Apollo.

I wanted to call my parents, but I was wrapped up in the glow of history.

TRAYVON

"Why do so many black superheroes wear hoods?" Deshaun asked his mother.

The kid was precocious, she knew, but wasn't six too young for that kind of truth? Still, she knew the world would one day force her hand.

Maybe she would start with the Skittles and the Arizona tea.

SHUFFLE BALL CHANGE

It was the scuffed up Capezios that did it for Linda. They'd been built up with taps—like Savion Glover's. If the shoes'd been even close to new, she wouldn't have given her another look.

It was something about dancers that did it for her, and this was no exception.

A BOWL OF YEP-YEP

Teddy's cupboard only contained a handful of seasonings—seasoned salt, lemon pepper, Worcestershire sauce, and hot sauce—but with those ingredients his cooking became legendary in Barkley Hall at Ellison-Wright College, where a framed picture of him still hangs fondly in the corridor of the third floor, next to Tupac.

I REALLY WANT TO WRITE ON HER PURPLE WALL

She'd waited quite a bit of time before she showed it to me, but when she finally did, I found myself completely mesmerized, unable to think about anything else. Then she eagerly invited me in—and I knew there was no way I could possibly deny myself this one thing.

AMAZING STORIES

I remember, as a child, watching *Amazing Stories* and seeing Christopher Lloyd in a bathrobe, running down a dark street carrying his own severed head. It was all I could talk about at school the next day. I knew then that I wanted to write those kinds of stories, too.

FUGA HACIA ADELANTE

(AFTER CÉSAR AIRA)

The Argentinian writer sat down and wrote a page every day, the words gradually transforming into something completely different from their beginnings, until finally an odd, yet universal, novel emerged from its disparate pieces, just poems and landscapes and zombies and ice cream and ghosts and clones of Carlos Fuentes.

SHIFTING PERSPECTIVES

"*E*lizabeth would learn many years later that she'd given birth to a baby *only a mother could love.*"

Now close your eyes. Seriously. Close your eyes.

Did you assume the mother in this story was white?

Tell the truth. I won't judge you.

Oh, you didn't?

Good. Now you're learning.

GROCERIES

They accidentally run into each other at the neighborhood grocery store, their toddlers in tow. Their kids begin to play with each other instinctively.

They know their kids could have been siblings, but instead their kids are strangers.

They take this notion home with them, buried deep beneath their groceries.

THE DOPPELGÄNGER

Three months after his daughter had died, Braxton discovered a spitting image of Laura working at a Forever 21. For months he walked past the store, until one day it went out of business and he never saw the girl again.

He took this loss even harder than the first.

NOSTALGIA

In the hours between the bachelorette party and the wedding ceremony, Jill did her best to hold on to all the memories of her life as a single woman, those amazing times in San Juan, Kingston, Cozumel, and New Orleans.

Approaching the church, she instructed the chauffeur to keep driving.

THE HAIRCUT

*J*ustin had never cut anyone else's hair, so when he got stuck trying to blend a fade, he politely excused himself to go watch instructional videos on YouTube, while his customer waited patiently in the barber chair, attempting to convince himself that he had not just made a huge mistake.

THE BEJESUS DOCTOR

Cori figured the bejesus was located in the center of the chest, since her mother always grabbed there and said, "You scared the bejesus out of me!" whenever Cori'd jump out of the hamper to surprise her.

When Cori grew up to become a cardiologist, she would save many bejesuses.

WHITE STATION, MISSISSIPPI

ardly anyone in the church knew that Deacon Johnny Lee Williams had been a bluesman back in his day, grinding his hips while blowing harp, downing rotgut by the gallon. But occasionally Sister Lulabelle Stewart, who had been around the block a few times herself, would wink at him knowingly.

A MUSEUM OF ASSES

The museum was full of portraits of asses. Asses of world leaders, entertainers, inventors, scholars, doctors, clergy, and athletes filled the walls. Some hairy, some bald, some freckled, some dimpled. The photographer was making a statement about something, we all knew, but none of us could quite figure out what.

SETTING THE RECORD STRAIGHT

Not a lot of people really know or understand just how long Rapunzel's dreadlocks really were. And they were strong, too! Prince Charming weighed a good 300 pounds, I tell you. I'm just saying that if we're going to tell her story, we should put some respect on her name.

MOST LIKELY TO SUCCEED

There was hardly any debate among the recent graduates that Gregory had acted in porn movies. Where they remained divided, however, was whether or not the word "star" should be attached to him, since the most voracious connoisseurs of porn among them had never spotted him in anything of note.

A SMALL ALTERATION?

*V*ernon was surprised to see the portrait his ex-girlfriend had painted of him featured in her new *Hi-Fructose* magazine spread. The nude painting was just as he remembered it, except his penis was smaller.

At first assuming revenge, he gradually realized that maybe she hadn't changed the painting after all.

A PLEASANT ROUTINE

Years after her own children had grown up and moved out, Betsy continued to rise at six, then make a hearty breakfast. And at seven-thirty, she watched the kids across the street board the number 45, headed across town to the memory of a school her children had once attended.

COME HOME

"No one even begs anymore," she sang.

It was just a catchy lyric in a song she enjoyed listening to. Yet, she had allowed her man to come back, sans begging, because Anderson .Paak knew that most men didn't have to. Not when they could play off of her loneliness.

PURPLE

After Grandad's funeral, the family went through his things looking for keepsakes and things to donate. My little sister was the one who discovered the Prince t-shirts. No one even knew he was a fan.

Now when I hear "Purple Rain," I try to imagine my grandfather smiling, singing along.

A VILLAGE ON FIRE

The dragon had burned the village to the ground. All that remained was the old stone well. Still, the villagers gathered at the well and rebuilt the village, brick by brick.

No longer afraid, the villagers went off to slay the dragon.

They would feast off its fear for weeks.

MEMORIES OF ORVIETO

They walked hand-in-hand beneath a purple parasol, down a cobblestone path that ran between two stone buildings, their blue shutters blossoming like spring gentians.

Decades later, that memory would come to mind when she laid him to rest on a small hill in Durham, his grave blanketed by soft snow.

THE THINGS LIBRARIANS NOTICE

For years Veronica watched the man amble into the library and pull out a copy of *The Catcher in the Rye*. Although she'd never read it, she was aware of the lore surrounding it.

Then one day the man stopped coming.

His absence bothered her more than she'd ever admit.

WHAT IS "WE LOVE YOU, ALEX"

When she first confronted things in the story collection that she didn't already know, she skipped over them. Then one day she decided to google those things and discovered she enjoyed the collection that much more.

Once she finished the book, she decided to apply for a spot on Jeopardy.

THE STRANGE MUSEUM

The museum was a cabinet of curiosities bearing tchotchkes from the literary greats: a shotgun casing from Hemingway, an oven dial from Plath, a stone from Woolf.

Hundreds of thousands of writers lined up for miles to see these objects, secretly wondering if they would one day contribute one themselves.

THANK YOU FOR VISITING THE STRANGE MUSEUM

PLEASE EXIT THROUGH THE GIFT SHOP

ACKNOWLEDGMENTS

A version of the following stories have been previously published:

"Ode to an Olivetti" (*50-Word Stories*), "The Motive" (*50-Word Stories*), "Dancing in the Light" (*50-Word Stories*), "The Story They Would One Day Tell Their Children" (*50-Word Stories*), "An Epilogue" (*50-Word Stories*), "How to Train a Beast" (*50-Word Stories*), "He's Coming" (*50-Word Stories*), "Until the End of Time" (*50-Word Stories*), "Purple" (*50-Word Stories*), "Hitchhikers" (*Speculative 66*), "Behind His Back" (*50-Word Stories*), "More Robot, Please" (*Blink-Ink*), "Hickory" (*50-Word Stories*), "Hunting Nightmares" (*50-Word Stories*), "The Smile" (*50-Word Stories*), "The Monster Inside" (*Paragraph Planet*), and "The Monster" (*50-Word Stories*).

I would like to thank the editors of the aforementioned journals, especially Tim Sevenhuysen of *50-Word Stories*, who has given me a platform for exploring this literary form.

I have drawn a great deal of inspiration from these writers, all of whom saw fit to explore writing at very short lengths: Lydia Davis, Diane Williams, Bob Thurber, Grant Faulkner, John Edgar Wideman, Desiree Cooper, Ernest Hemingway, and all of the writers who have seen the benefit in writing stories that can be read in under a minute.

A special thanks to Haruki Murakami, whose novella *The Strange Library* inspired the title of this book.

I would also like to thank Torrey H. Walker, Sabin P. Duncan, Mitchell Davis and the Biblio-Labs team, and all the librarians who continue to make a difference in our communities. Your collective support has gone a long way.

Finally, but by no means least, I would like to thank my wife, Lauren, and daughter, Zoë, for loving me and encouraging me to follow my dreams.

ALSO BY RAN WALKER

B-Sides and Remixes

30 Love: A Novel

Mojo's Guitar: A Novel / (Il était une fois Morris Jones)

Afro Nerd in Love: A Novella

The Keys of My Soul: A Novel

The Race of Races: A Novel

The Illest: A Novella

Bessie, Bop, or Bach: Collected Stories

Four Floors (with Sabin Prentis)

Black Hand Side: Stories

White Pages: A Novel

She Lives in My Lap

Reverb

Work-In-Progress

Daykeeper

Most of My Heroes Don't Appear On No Stamps

Portable Black Magic

ABOUT THE AUTHOR

(IN 50 WORDS)

Ran Walker is the author of eighteen books. He is the winner of the 2019 Indie Author of the Year and 2019 BCALA Fiction Ebook Awards. He teaches creative writing at Hampton University and lives with his wife and daughter in Virginia. He can be reached via his website, www.ranwalker.com.